thank you

Cover Artist: Roaa bb.

Sometimes, it's hard closing a chapter, this is somewhat worse, closing a book before reaching the end there will be no end just wishful dreaming and hoping

I don't consider myself a poet, and what I write is not poetry, Its words and feelings not of rhyme but of longing, endless longing, words vomited on a page just so you could read me, just so you can understand that I am ever so pathetic, waiting for you to reach out, hold me, tell me it'll be okay.

'Inspire me'
He said
'Look me in the eyes
And show me your true beauty.'

You are the burning eminent sky
I am but the humble earth that tries to reach you,
through mountains and hills and quakes and shakes.
I just look up, and I burn.

And just like that, all my worries disappeared, and so did you.

His gaze represented my universe, empty and cold.
Desolate.

Words simply can't express the way you make me feel. No sun, no matter how bright, could warm my heart as much as you.

Your love grew a rose in the bitter cold.

<u>Trabzon,   2023</u>

I saw the sea in a different way.
I saw the waves embrace, the way your hands clasped mine.
I saw the tides come and go, the way you'd always come back to me.
I see you in every form: water, earth, tears and more. For no depth nor
distance can separate you from me.

And the comfort I feel when our hands brush.

<u>Andromeda</u>

The stars are jealous of your eyes.
They burn with love, possessiveness and passion.
You have burnt them more than me.
I have never missed such pain before.

The ocean's depth pales beside the depths in your eyes.

Maybe it was love
Or
Maybe it was our cursed fate

As the breeze stirs, it lifts the butterflies,
Awakening with our shared gaze.

He looked at me and I forgot how to breathe.

Diamonds

In your presence, the diamonds that gracefully adorn my neck, Sparkling with their costly gleam and elegant finesse, Seem to lose their lustre, their brilliance dimmed, For when I gaze upon you, their value fades into nothingness. Your radiance outshines the most precious stones.

Winter days and summer nights with you is heaven in my eyes.

His love was the rain that grew a garden in my heart.

My new favourite poem is *you*.

<u>Lost</u>

The thought of losing you was unbearable, so in that fear, I lost myself. I let my soul slip away, caught in the frenzy of keeping you close. My identity, once clear and strong, became a shadow, faded and blurred in the background of my desperate attempts to hold onto you. It was as if, in trying to grasp onto your presence, I let go of my own, forgetting that in love, one should not lose oneself but rather find a new depth within.

What good is hope when you stare at me like

a stranger.

Sometimes all I want to do is pinch myself to remember that I am not in a dream because;

My dear, you are too good to be true.

I couldn't write poetry, i forgot the feeling of love.

One look into your soul and I was positively addicted
to your very being.

And suddenly I crave Thursday mornings with you.

<u>Tryhard</u>

I spent hours playing your games, hoping I'd see you again; each moment spent learning the game was a silent wish, a quiet longing for a connection, a chance to be alongside you.

The way our hands intertwined,
the way you looked me in the eyes
reminds me that true happiness still exists.

My poetry is my undying gift of pure love and grave honesty to you.

In a few more days, our eyes will meet once again.

Tempest

Your presence is like a peaceful storm, an unending paradox that defies nature's rules-a whirlwind of tranquillity where madness dances with love. Like the gentle rumble of distant thunder, your voice brings a calm that I can't help but wonder. In your eyes, I see the lightning's flash- bright, electric, but never brash. Around you, the air changes, charged with an energy that rearranges. You are the rain that soothes and heals, the wind that whispers and reveals. In your arms, I find shelter, a haven from life's hate. Your touch, soft as a drizzle, yet potent as the storm's crescendo. With you, I embrace the tempest's heart, finding in its eye a world apart.

My heart beats briefly but only so I can write for you.

<u>Youth</u>

Your laughter, warmth, and the way you hold my hand will be the source of youth, keeping the sparkle in my eyes and the bounce in my step, even when our steps are a little slower.

My eyes water at the fact I won't be able to see you in a year.

Sometimes I wonder if you still remember my voice
as it called out your name.

Stories of happily ever after clouds my eyes And when I look at you, I realize it's with you.

In fragmented whispers, the concept of 'perfect' disintegrates.
Under your gaze, it's a relic, a shadow, an echo.

I really miss the way your eyes gleam.

<u>Knots and loops</u>

Even as stars burn out above,
And skies turn to the deepest black, Through the passage of time and age,
My heart will forever hold a track.

I will, and always, without end,
In waking moments and dreams so true, Find my thoughts returning in a
loop, Ever and always, back to you.

.

Every time you pass me in the hall; I feel alive.

You told her you loved her yet you're holding me instead.

My poetry is my heart crying out ink as I think of you.

Sanctuary

Your voice, a gentle melody, cascades through the quiet of my thoughts, weaving a tapestry of tranquil dreams. It's as if each word you speak is a brushstroke in an unseen masterpiece, painting landscapes of serenity in the canvas of my mind. In the timbre of your voice, I find a sanctuary, a soothing balm that quiets the chaos of the day. It's like a soft, persistent rain on a spring morning, nurturing the earth and inviting new life to awaken.

Maybe the world just doesn't want us together?

Maybe it just wasn't ~~me~~ who was meant for you.

What is love but hopeless dreams and broken promises?

Maybe you were just a childish fantasy

And suddenly I was starting to hate the word 'Love'.

Who are you to litter the ground with the shards of my heart?

<u>Quiet</u>

There's a resonance in this silence, a melody that plays beneath the surface of our everyday chatter. It's like a secret conversation, one that doesn't require the clutter of words. In your presence, I find a comfort in the unsaid, a peace in the unarticulated.

Your words do not interest me anymore.

The way your eyes bore into my soul is the way my words go unsaid.

You were my everything And you still are but less.

Maybe if I said it, it'll come true

Between the lines

In the silence left by my last sad story, I find the space to breathe, to dream, and to write anew. For poetry is not just the language of sorrow but the voice of life in all its shades, waiting to be captured in words that dance between the lines.

They said give it a day, it's been 8 months.

See the light in your eyes it tells me; if only.

Lately all I could think of is how much I want you out of my head.

My veins that are pumped with ink,
And I bleed every word,
Every day for you.

<u>Emptiness</u>

In a dimly lit room, where the curtains never quite open, an unclosed book lies heavy on a dust-laden desk. Its pages once eagerly turned, are now stagnant, each line a testament to a love that once burned fiercely, now extinguished. The inkwell beside it, dry and barren, echoes the emptiness that has settled in.

I can't help falling in love with you with every second that passes.

The way you talk with sparkles in your eyes is my forever midnight sky.

Waking up to see you sleeping beside me on the fine silky fabric of the blanket is my haven.

Because I could not love for me I loved for him

The gentle feeling of his rough touch on my soft skin.

The way your voice hangs in my head
Makes me wish I never even met you

Magic

Your love is a magic that does not vanish with the morning mist but grows stronger with each passing day. It's an alchemy that turns my fears into fortitude, my doubts into dreams, and my ordinary life into an extraordinary journey. With you, I believe in magic, for you are the miracle that changed my world.

Without you in my mind I have no more words to write.

You're the blood that pumps in my pen.

You're the ink that runs in my blood

You're the thought that is stuck in my head.

As long as you're happy with her; I'm happy alone.

Lies

How can you say you love me?
How dare you say you love me?
How could you say you love me?

How could you make me feel loved?
How dare you make me feel loved?
How can you make me feel loved?

Because deep down, you confused love with loneliness And it shows.

Once again I start to hate the word 'love'.

I believed that you meant something to me, You left
And I cried And I moved on.

I am grateful for the hate you have given me,
Now i have hate to give back to the world.

Sometimes I feel your eyes on me,
but I still don't feel a single thing.

You'll come back to me I'm sure;
but I know for a fact I won't let you in again

The sea isn't blue
And your love for me was not pure

The skies are black The clouds are grey
The sky is my heart The clouds are my eyes
And nothing will ever be the same.

I write as much as I love and as much as I hurt.
My heart aches.

I usually forgive and forget,
but I lost hope in forgiving
and I stopped forgetting.

After you tied my heart together and made me one again?
You started ripping apart my threads and cutting your ties with me.

<u>Why?</u>

Even now, after all this time, you ask, "Why?" But your voice carries a different tone, tinged with the remnants of heartache. Your smile doesn't quite reach your eyes; it's more a brave attempt to mask the pain, a façade of acceptance over a wound still raw. The question lingers in the air, a reflection of your struggle to make peace with the unexplained, the lost, the changed. It's a quiet surrender to the mysteries of life that leave us broken yet still searching for some semblance of understanding in the chaos of lost love.

You still have love in your eyes, and I'm still alone.

It's been 3 weeks
and I have never been more at peace with myself.
I finally know who I am,
I am nobody to you.

I worry even with all my words that you are reading this but not the way I want you to.

I wear my stones in desperation for your eyes.

Sometimes I question why I am incapable of love,
and then I remember you.

I can't love
I won't love Yet
I want love

Ink and Blood

I had thought the bleeding had ceased, that the wounds of the past had finally healed. But then you came along, unknowingly tearing at the fragile seams of my mended heart. And so, the wound reopens, not with blood, but with ink-a torrent of emotions and unspoken words pouring out onto the page. Each drop of ink is a piece of my heart, a testament to the pain and love that still lingers within. My chest, once healed, now bleeds again, but this time, it's through the words I write, a bittersweet symphony of memories and longing, penned with the ink of a heart still raw and yearning.

If you are as untouchable as you say,
why do you crave my touch?

You are the after party of my soul.

You make me lust after love.

I am the rays of the sun and you are the moonlight of perfection

I wonder what makes her so special, her beauty? Or her lack of a brain?

<u>Melancholy</u>

Each time I see your ring resting on my tabletop, a wave of melancholic sadness washes over me. The sight of it, solitary and still, is a silent whisper of a past that is both cherished and mourned, a token of a bond that once was, now resting quietly in the aftermath of goodbye.

Who throws away diamonds for rhinestones?
Only you.

Death didn't seem too bad after I met you.

I see you seeing me and yet
I don't see me seeing you.

A blank page is all I can manage when you're in my mind, you make me speechless beyond belief.

The leaves rustled softly, whispering secrets of growth and renewal. In this garden, resurrected by the simple act of our hands coming together.

My words don't interest you, yet I still write to you daily.

You aren't mad that he sent me all those things;
you're mad because I saw you for who you really are.

My ink dries,
taking the shape of my longing towards you.
Slowly but surely, it runs out.

Your hair,
your lips,
your very being,
makes me want to fall even deeper in love with you

The sound of silence opposes the serenity of my feelings.

You said perfection doesn't exists but I found perfection in all your imperfections.

You're the first I can't write about, because you're the first I've ever felt nervous around.

I worry about you reading my art, I worry about you judging me.

I want go cloud watching with you and show you how pretty the morning sky is;
yet it cannot compare to your midnight sky eyes.

I'm sorry I'm not what you wanted.

I wonder
I wonder
I wonder
I will always wonder

Through blue and pink,
Cotton and silk.
My flowers ink
Never wilting, it stays distinct.

No more love poems for you; I don't think it should be a thing anymore.

Its 2:22 am and I want to go to bed
but I can't cause I'm thinking of you instead.

Why did I think it was gonna be different?
Why did I think you were gonna be different?
It will never be different.

I don't know if I should send you these words or just burn them, it's a lost cause either way.

It was true; you are a childish fantasy.
And I still dream like the fool I am.

In a cage, I dwell, no escape I find,
Your steel words are a trap of the mind.
Your kisses, like locks, hold me tight,
A captive to your embrace, day and nigt.

Would you happen to even think about me anymore? I wonder if you found someone new. I bet you don't, and I'll be here waiting and crying my ass over you.

I wonder if you dream of me like I dream of you

As I waited for your touch and your embrace,
the seasons started to change.

Fuck it I'm still so fucking in love with you.

I honestly don't know if I should still give you it, will you laugh about it with your friends? Or throw it away without reading it? Or I hope I hope and I hope you keep it and you read it over and over and over again.

This is more of a diary than a poetry book,
it's hard to make things rhyme when you're sad.

Walking in a crowd, and I hear your voice,
I look in the mirror and see your hands nestled in my hair,
I put on my clothes and see the ones we left on the floor.
Time travels quickly, yet my memory of you never seems to fade away.

I write for you but not for your eyes to skim,
I write for you but not for your mouth to read,
I write for you but not for you,
I write for your soul that's tied with mine.

I wonder if you read my old poems like I do,
every word dedicated to you,
I wonder when someone will do the same for me.

I write scarcely, yet I yearn for you endlessly

In soft blankets, On fluffy pillows, I dream of you, Endlessly.

I see you in rings and ink,
I hear you in the wind and songs. I feel you in my dreams,
Holding me with soft yawns.

I have everything yet I feel more alone than ever.

I wait for you in tears and thoughts,
I wait for you in sobs and dreams,
I wait for you in death and life,
I wait for only you.

I played with ropes when I was young,
and I always thought I'd be tying the knot with someone I loved
but I don't know anymore.

Our love grows and entwines like vines in a lush, sun- dappled garden. Each tendril, tender and exploratory, reaches out, seeking each other.

In dreams, your laughter softly weaves,
Yet morning breaks and my empty heart grieves.

I walk along the rows of flowers,
Glancing at their green column.
Wondering when I'll be strong enough
To finally bloom just like them.

In old texts, I seek your trace,
Through time-worn frames, I see your face,
In quiet cafes, where memories brew,
I savour moments spent with you.

I find it hard to write,
It's like you killed the poet within me.

My love, an ocean
Slowly moving in and out
Sometimes low and sometimes high
But always cold and salty.

I'm scared that you'll read this, and you'd block me, and I'd lose you forever.

Sweet, cold tea,
Hot, bitter coffee,
Your hand in mine,
Life feels cozy.

Each page is a testament to my longing, a silent witness to the love that still lingers in my heart.

<u>Broken wings</u>

I remember how I stood by you in your bleakest hours. It was a time when your world seemed to crumble, and I was there, holding you up, mending the cracks with words of encouragement and hands ready to catch you. I watched as you pieced yourself back together, drawing strength from the support I freely gave.

But there's a bittersweet twist in our story. As you began to flourish, finding your footing and your smile again, the path you chose took you away from me. It's a strange feeling, knowing that the strength you gained from our shared struggles became the wings you used to fly away. You spread those wings wide, showing your best self to a world that never saw your struggles, a world that wasn't me.

I wish I was a cloud.

I'll send you this book, and if you've read this far,
please know that I'll still care no matter what you do to me.

I'm writing so much in so little time, there's just so much I want to tell you.

Well for starters, I really like love your voice, it's just so fucking cute
(btw it's 3:13 am)

I also love the way you hate my jokes; it makes me happy when I see you roll your eyes or when you squinch your eyes shut.

I also love the way you listen and care for me, especially when I rant about my physics,
I doubt you can remember; that's never your strong suit.

I also loved your hair,
it's a shame you shaved it,
it was such a pretty brown

I honestly don't know why I'm writing this; I just can't help this; I really, really fucking love you, but you don't feel the same way, and that's okay.

I don't know what to say anymore.
I probably embarrassed myself to death already.

I'm honestly terrified of giving this to you.

Just please be gentle with me and my heart;
I don't know how much more I can take.

I don't mind if we stay friends, as long as you're in my life.

It's sad but honestly I really don't wanna end this, I'm too fucking scared to end this.

I'm also scared that I'll send you this, but I would've forgotten to tell you something.

I'm scared that I'll give you my everything and I'll get it given back again.

i miss you

always,

Printed in Great Britain
by Amazon

36950207R20098